THE LITTLE WITCH

WHO WANTED TO BE GOOD

First published in 2021
by Kristina Cooper
with What's Your Story, an imprint
of New Life Publishing, Luton, UK

British Library Cataloguing in Publication Data
A catalogue record for this book is available
from the British Library.

ISBN   978 1 912237 27 2

Illustrations and front cover design
by Jessica Cooper and used with permission.

Typesetting by goodnewsbooks.co.uk
Printed and bound in the UK

The Little Witch Who Wanted To Be Good

by Kristina Cooper

illustrated by Jessica Cooper

Dedicated to Granny Maud,
for being such a great mother
and grandmother to the Cooper clan

and to

Miss Kirsten, from Eaton House,
The Manor Girls' School in Clapham
and her class of F3 (2013), Lottie, Minxie,
Laura, Eleanor, Robyn, Maddie, Anya,
Isobel, Rosie, Rhea, Alexandra and Eva.
Thanks to your encouragement
and feedback, I didn't give up.
That this book has now been published
is in no small way thanks to you all.

(See back pages for their comments!)

CONTENTS

Chapter One

Esmeralda
Wants to be a Readie

O nce upon a time there was a little girl called Esmeralda. She came from a long line of witches and lived with her Aunt Agatha and Aunt Hepzibah in a little cottage on the edge of a dark wood.

She loved her aunts but she was very lonely because she had nobody to play with except her aunts' cat, Philbert, who was very bad tempered.

Near her house was the village school. Esmeralda so wanted to go to school like the other girls and boys but she wasn't allowed to because she was special.

'Why am I special?' asked Esmeralda.

'Because you are a witch,' explained Aunt Hepzibah, 'and we don't want you picking up bad habits from the boys and girls in the village.'

Poor Esmeralda was very disappointed. Every

morning she had lessons by herself where she learnt to be a proper witch and cast spells.

She learnt how to turn milk sour and make babies cry. She learnt how to make people feel itchy all over just for the fun of it. She learnt how to turn good little children into frogs. And to never say 'thank you' or 'please.'

Poor Esmeralda. She didn't enjoy her lessons.

One day she asked her Aunt Agatha, 'Why do you only teach me to do nasty things? I want to be good,' she said.

'What!' shrieked her aunts *in unison**. 'What would your parents say if they could hear you now? After all we have done for you, teaching you to be a proper witch and now you want to be good like an ordinary child.'

Esmeralda began to cry because she loved her aunts and didn't want to upset them but she so longed to be good and kind.

One day she was studying about her great uncle Horace, who had turned a troop of Readies into a flock of sheep because they had been having too much fun.

'What are Readies?' asked Esmeralda.

'Ug...' said Aunt Hepzibah looking disgusted. 'They are horrible little girls who try to be kind and thoughtful and do good things every day. They help old ladies across the road, they do their homework and help their mothers with the washing up.'

'Yes,' added Aunt Agatha. 'They even put their pyjamas under their pillows and clean their teeth!'

3

'Imagine!' said Aunt Hepzibah. 'All in all *thoroughly**
unpleasant girls and to be avoided.'

Esmeralda didn't say anything but she decided
secretly that she would rather like to be a Readie and
that it sounded rather fun.

One day she was in the garden practicing her spells
on Philbert the cat. One minute she turned him into
a frog and the next into a cow. Poor Philbert got very
confused. No wonder he got snappy as he didn't
know whether to moo or to croak or to miaow.

Suddenly Esmeralda heard the sound of laughing
and she saw two little girls in red outfits coming up
the lane. She was so excited. She knew her aunts
would be very cross if they knew she was talking to
them, but she couldn't resist it.

'Hello,' she said. 'Hello,' replied the girls, who were called Angela and Clare.

'Are you Readies?' Esmeralda asked.

'Yes', they replied. 'We belong to the Readie troop in the village.' We are in the Bumble Bee pack. That's why we both have that bumble bee badge sewn onto our sleeves.

'Why are you wearing that badge that looks like a ladybird?' asked Esmeralda.

'That's our Readie emblem,' explained Angela. 'It means we are fully fledged Readies and have a done a hundred good deeds!'

'A hundred!' Esmeralda was impressed. 'What kind of good deeds?' she asked.

'Helping with the washing up, fetching my grandpa's newspaper from the shop,' said Clare.

'Making get well cards for people who are sick, being kind to people who are lonely,' added Angela. 'And making lots of cups of tea for my mum,' finished Clare. 'Can you make a cup of tea?'

'No,' said Esmeralda, 'but I can turn milk sour.'

'That's not very useful,' said the girls.

'I know,' said Esmeralda, 'but I'm a witch and I only know how to do horrible things.'

'Poor you,' said the girls. 'Would you like us to teach you to make a cup of tea?'

'Oh yes,' said Esmeralda, feeling rather naughty. What would her aunts say?

So Esmeralda went off with Angela and Clare to the Readie Meeting in the village hall. Here she met all the other Readies and stood in line with them as they recited together the Readie Promise:

'I promise to always be ready to be generous, kind, honest, cheerful and courageous. I promise to help others, to love God and serve my community,' they said in unison.

Esmeralda had never heard anything so lovely before.

During the evening session, Esmeralda learnt not only how to make a cup of tea but also to bake some delicious fairy cakes, with cherries on the top, and to say 'please' and 'thank you' when she was asking for things.

'You've done really well,' said Chief Ladybird, who was the head of the village troop and was the the class teacher for year 3. 'You must come back again Esmeralda,' she said.

Esmeralda was so excited but she was also a little worried at what her aunts would say if they found out where she had been so she *sneaked** into the house as quietly as possible.

When she arrived home, however, she found her aunts were nowhere to be seen. They were both in bed with flu.

'I feel terrible,' said Aunt Hepzibah. 'I feel worse,' said

8

Aunt Agatha, who always had to be more important than her younger sister. 'My head hurts,' said Aunt Hepzibah. 'My nose is blocked up,' said Aunt Agatha.

'Can't you do a spell to make yourselves well?' asked Esmeralda. 'No,' the pair grumbled. 'We can only do bad things.'

Esmeralda decided that the best thing she could do in the circumstances was to make them both a nice cup of hot tea and give them some of the fairy cakes she had made.

Her aunts wanted to be cross with her but they were too ill to make a fuss and they had to admit that the tea was really *thirst-quenching** and the cakes were delicious.

The whole week her aunts were in bed, Esmeralda looked after them. She ran up and down the stairs all day making them cups of tea and *plumping** their pillows and stroking their foreheads and generally being helpful and kind.

Clare and Angela also popped in to see how Esmeralda was managing and they went to the shops to buy groceries when supplies started getting low. By the time Esmeralda's aunts were better, they were beginning to wonder if maybe being nice and kind and helpful wasn't better than being wicked and nasty.

Thus, her aunts decided that maybe they would let Esmeralda become a Readie after all as long as she promised to not become TOO good!

Chapter Two

Esmeralda and the
Beauty Spells

E smeralda was bored. It was raining and the Readies were away on camp but she hadn't been allowed to go and felt very glum.

'Why don't you do something useful?' said Aunt Agatha.

'You could make me a cup of tea, if you like?' said Aunt Hepzibah.

'Oh don't encourage her to be good,' said Aunt Agatha sharply. 'Why don't you go upstairs and practice some spells. Just because we are allowing you to be a Readie we don't want you slipping behind in your proper education. When I was your age I could make a whole herd of milking cows dry!'

Esmeralda didn't think that sounded very nice, particularly as she was a Readie now and wanted to do good deeds. So instead she said, 'I know, I'll go and tidy up the books in the spell library.'

Aunt Agatha *made a grimace**. Esmeralda could be very trying but at least it would stop her from finding some other good deed to do.

Sidney, Esmeralda's pet spider jumped into her pocket because he wanted to do some good deeds too.

To be honest, however, he wasn't very much help as he kept *scampering** about and making silver webs in corners where Esmeralda had just dusted.

13

As Esmeralda stretched up to a high corner, one of the book of spells came tumbling down with a clatter. Esmeralda bent to pick it up. On the cover in beautiful gothic handwriting was written 'Grizelda's Beauty Spells'.

Intrigued*, Esmeralda opened up the book. There were spells for everything. There were spells to remove warts and pimples, and to have silken hair, and longer eyelashes, and clear skin and shining eyes.

Now here for once was a really useful book, she thought, with nice spells, worth doing to help people. Just at that moment Aunt Agatha came in to check on her. Esmeralda showed her the book. 'Who was Grizelda?' she asked, 'Was she a relation?'

'Yes' said Aunt Agatha. 'She was a distant cousin, who lived a few centuries ago. She was the most beautiful woman in the land and ended up marrying the king.'

'Wow', said Esmeralda, impressed to think they had royalty in their family tree.

'Yes,' continued Aunt Agatha. 'But unfortunately the king had been married before and poor Grizelda had a very unpleasant step daughter called Snow White. The girl was very pretty, which was very stressful for Grizelda. She was always having to find new beauty spells so she could keep her title as the most beautiful woman in the land. In the end it all became too much for her and she decided the best thing would be to get rid of the girl. So she told her trusted huntsman to take Snow White into the forest and kill her. But he was very deceitful and didn't do as he was told.'

'Shocking!' tutted Aunt Hepzibah. 'What happened then?' asked Esmeralda, intrigued. 'The girl moved into a flat share with seven dwarfs in a forest,' *interjected** Aunt Hepzibah, as she liked to show that she knew all the gossip. Aunt Agatha looked crossly at her sister and continued firmly, 'I can't remember the whole story. But it ended badly for Grizelda. Her step daughter married a prince and Grizelda got so angry she died of rage.'

'Gosh!' said Esmeralda. 'But the good thing that came out of it all,' said Aunt Hepzibah, 'was that we inherited her beauty spells, which have been a real money spinner for the family down the ages, as women always want to look more beautiful than they are.'

'Can I borrow the book and practice some of these spells?' asked Esmeralda.

'Of course,' said Aunt Agatha, delighted at long last that Esmeralda was showing some interest in the family business. Esmeralda excitedly took the book up to her room. She thumbed the pages and wondered what she would like to start with. She decided she would practice on Philbert and *enticed** him up to the room with a saucer of milk.

Poor Philbert – he had his fur curled and straighted, turned *different hues** from deep auburn to golden blonde and had his lashes lengthened, which he didn't like at all.

Just at that moment Esmeralda looked out of the window and coming along the path were Angela and Clare, her friends from the Readies, who had just returned from camp. She was delighted to see them and shouted down for them to come up and see her, as she wanted to hear all about the camp. Philbert took the opportunity to make himself scarce.

When the girls had finished telling Esmeralda all the wonderful things they had done, they noticed the book that she had out. 'What's that book about?' said Clare.

'It's a book of beauty spells that I have been practicing,' replied Esmeralda. 'Really… how exciting,' said Angela seizing the book and flicking through the pages.

'Golden hair… I have always wanted to have long

golden hair. Can you do a spell to change my hair?' she said. 'I hate mine.'

Esmeralda had always liked Angela's red hair, and she wasn't quite sure what Angela's mother was going to say, but she didn't want to disappoint her friend, so she agreed.

'Wow! How exciting. What do I have to do?' said Angela.

'Just sit there,' said Esmeralda trying to appear more confident than she felt. Taking her wand in her right hand she carefully read out the spell. In an instant Angela's red curls had become long golden fairy tale locks.

Angela looked in the mirror. The hair was really beautiful but it didn't quite go with her round freckled face and she didn't look like the beautiful princess she hoped she would.

'Oh… is there a spell for freckles?' she asked. 'I want a lovely peaches and cream complexion like Gloria in our class. I can't have golden hair and a face like this.'

Esmeralda could see there was some point in this, as it didn't quite look right.

'And while you are at it, could you give me some really lovely cornflower blue eyes?' said Angela, deciding she might as well go for the full princess look.

Esmeralda searched through the book until she found the page on skin tones. It was a while before Angela was satisfied that she had exactly the right honey tone.

Clare, meanwhile, was getting a bit impatient because there were lots of things she wanted to change about herself too.

'To begin with,' she said. 'You have to do something about my ears.' Clare had sweet ears but they did stick out a bit through her hair. Esmeralda had noticed this but she thought it was rather cute and made Clare, Clare. But she realised if she had given Angela a make-over it wouldn't be fair to leave out Clare.

'I want really long eye lashes too,' said Clare, 'and dark eyes and red lips and black hair.' Esmeralda did as she was told and before long she was faced with two extremely beautiful girls, who looked liked princesses from a fairy tale. But they weren't Clare and Angela.

The girls, however, were delighted. 'Will we stay like this?' asked Angela, concerned that all this beauty might suddenly disappear.

Esmeralda consulted the spell book. 'It seems as if there is a trial period of 24 hours when you have the opportunity to go back to the way you were. But after that it is permanent.'

'I can't wait to show everyone,' said Clare.

'Oh no, look at the time,' said Angela. They were having so much fun they had forgotten the time. 'We must hurry home or our parents will be worried.'

The pair rushed down the path towards the village. On the way they met Chief Ladybird, the leader of the Readie troop, looking very anxious.

'Excuse me, have you seen two girls, one with red curly hair and one with brown hair?' she said. 'They have disappeared and we are very worried about them.'

Clare and Angela and smiled, 'It's us, Chief Ladybird. Clare and Angela', they said. But Esmeralda's spell had even changed their voices and they had princess voices too.

Chief Ladybird looked at them *quizzically**. 'What do you mean? You are not Angela and Clare. I have never seen either of you before. Do you know something about their disappearance?' she added suspiciously.

'It really is us,' the girls insisted.

But Chief Ladybird was having none of it. 'I haven't got time to talk nonsense with you. I have to find my girls,' and with that she rushed off in the direction of the village.

'We'd better hurry home, if people are looking for us,' said Clare. They both were starting to feel a bit uncomfortable. Things weren't turning out the way they expected.

When Clare got home she found her mother was sitting at the kitchen table crying. Clare rushed up to hug her. But her mother looked up startled.

'Who are you?' she said. 'It's me, mum,' said Clare.

'I have never seen you before in my life. What kind of cruel joke is this? My daughter and her friend are lost and there is a search party looking for them.'

Clare started crying herself. This was a nightmare. It was no fun looking like a princess if your friends and family didn't recognise you. Clare realised she wanted to go back to the way things were before.

She rushed out of the house and back towards the forest where Esmeralda lived. She met Angela at the gate.

'O Clare. I hate this new look,' said Angela. 'Even Angus my dog didn't know me and growled.'

'It's horrible, isn't it?' said Clare. 'I suddenly realised I like my life and being me, even if I do have sticking out ears.'

Esmeralda was delighted to see her two friends again.

'Please can you make another spell to turn us back to the way we were,' said Angela. 'We want to be ourselves again,' said Clare.

Fortunately the trial period of the spell was still valid and it was quite easy for Esmeralda to reverse the spell.

In a flash the two beautiful princesses disappeared and Angela and Clare returned. They both rushed to the mirror to look at themselves.

'O thank goodness,' they cried in unison.

'My freckles – they are back! And my hair!' said Angela with a smile of relief on her face.

'I never thought I would be pleased to see my sticky out ears, but I am,' said Clare. 'My mum told me that they are just like her mum's and I was so proud.'

Esmeralda was pleased too because she liked her friends just the way they were. As she put the spell book back on the shelf she decided that even good spells were perhaps best left alone.

Chapter Three

Esmeralda is Expelled

'How old are you on your next birthday, Esmeralda?' asked Aunt Agatha one day, quite out of the blue, as she was making some spider leg soup.

'Seven,' replied Esmeralda. She wondered why her aunt wanted to know, as she knew witches didn't believe in birthdays or giving other people presents.

'Hmm,' her aunt *mused**. 'I think it is about time you mixed with some witches of your own age.'

'Yes', agreed Aunt Hepzibah. 'We can't keep you at home all the time. I've heard there is a marvelous Academy for young witches near Littletoon Crag.'

'Witchthorn Academy has a wonderful reputation,' she enthused. 'The pupils are always fighting and using bad language in the playground. And they are taught to lie and steal and answer back.'

'Yes, wouldn't you like to be able to stare someone in

the eye and tell them a bare-faced lie?' said Aunt Agatha. 'You always turn red whenever you do anything wrong.'

Poor Esmeralda – she wanted to be good and thought the Witchthorn Academy for Young Witches sounded horrid, but what could she do? She was only a little witch and had to do what she was told.

'This is definitely the right thing,' said Aunt Agatha, taking out her goose quill pen to write to the headmistress. 'You've been spending far too much time with those dreadful Readies and have picked up far too many bad habits.'

'I thought you liked Clare and Angela,' said Esmeralda. Aunt Agatha looked guilty. 'Of course I don't,' she said hastily. 'I couldn't possible like good children like that. You just never know when they are going to be pleasant and suddenly say 'please' or 'thank you'. You know what that does to my nerves, to have good manners in the house! We are witches after all and have our reputations to think about.'

Esmeralda had warned the girls on several occasions about their language when they visited Cauldron Cottage but they would keep saying 'please' and 'thank

you' all the time and upsetting her aunts with their sunny smiles and helpfulness.

'Please don't bring them bunches of flowers when you come to visit or offer to fetch their slippers,' said Esmeralda, after one very trying visit. 'Can't you just pretend that they are old and boring.'

'We can't do that,' said Angela. 'We're Readies and we have to be nice to older ladies.'

'Yes,' agreed Clare, 'and anyway we think they are rather sweet, although they are always trying to be grumpy. We like them.'

No wonder with such *incorrigibly** good friends her aunts had decided to send her away from their influence, thought Esmeralda.

There was no avoiding it and at the next full moon poor Esmeralda sadly set off for the Witchthorn Academy in the next valley.

She could hear the children in the village school laughing and playing happily in the playground. 'Oh why had she been born a witch?' she thought to herself. She would so love to join them instead of having to go to the horrid Witchthorn Academy for Young Witches at Littletoon Crag.

The Witchthorn Academy was as bad as she had expected. When she arrived there was a mini-riot in the

playground and lots of shouting and crying. 'I want that,' yelled a rather unpleasant looking boy, as he stole a smaller child's break-time biscuit. 'But it's mine,' wailed the little boy.

'I am bigger than you so I can do what I want,' said the bully with an ugly sneer.

Esmeralda felt really sorry for the little boy and went over to comfort him. She remembered that the two chocolate biscuits Clare and Angela had given her were still in her pocket.

'Look', she said brightly, drying his tears with her handkerchief. 'I've got two chocolate biscuits. You can have one of these, if you want,' she said, offering the boy one of her biscuits.

'Oh thank you,' said the boy, gratefully taking it.

But unfortunately for Esmeralda, one of the teachers overheard her. 'You – the new girl – come over here!' she screeched. 'What do you mean by interfering when someone is bullying another child. And then having the *audacity** to share your biscuits too and getting him to use the 'thank you' word.' Do you know what we do here to children who share?' And with that she hauled poor Esmeralda off to the house-mistress for a telling off.

'I know this is your first day,' said Miss Scream, the house-mistress, peering down her spectacles, 'but this is not the sort of behaviour we expect at Witchthorn Academy. Sharing is absolutely forbidden here.'

To teach her a lesson, Esmeralda's lunch was confiscated and given to the bully, who smirked at her.

'Teacher's pet,' thought Esmeralda, but she didn't care. She knew she had done the right thing and she felt nice inside even if she knew she would be a bit hungry later.

'I think I had better send you to Miss Pincher's class, One Toad,' said Miss Scream. She is a very experienced teacher and I'm sure she will be able to sort you out and turn you into a proper little witch.'

One Toad had already started the first class of the day when Esmeralda arrived. They were learning how to say nasty things to people that really hurt them.

Miss Pincher was a rather plump witch with grey hair scraped into a bun, a pince-nez perched on a her nose and a disagreeable expression on her face.

'Now class, it is very important that if you want to upset people, you must find out what they feel sensitive about and then say nasty things about that. Can anyone give me an example?' she asked.

'Calling a fat person like Henry, 'fatty', said Hortense,

the class swot, as she pointed to a rather plump boy sitting at the back of the class. 'Exactly,' said Miss Pincher. 'Has anybody got any other examples?'

Henry blushed embarrassedly and retorted crossly. 'Hortense has got skinny legs…..skinny legs, skinny legs,' he chanted. Poor Hortense began to cry as she felt very sensitive about her thin legs and always wore thick tights to cover them up. She hated Henry Blob as he was always picking on her.

'Excellent, excellent,' said Miss Pincher. 'You see how easy it is once you get started. You can get all kinds of reactions from tears to anger. It is such fun.'

Esmeralda, however, didn't think it was very good fun. She didn't like to see people crying and upset or getting angry and being nasty to people. When the teacher wasn't looking she leaned over and whispered to Hortense, 'I don't think you've got skinny legs. I think you're very pretty and you have got lovely golden hair. Henry Blob only said that because you upset him. I think he secretly likes you.'

Hortense dried her tears and gave her a weak smile. 'do you think so?' she said. 'You're nice.' 'Why don't you go and say you are sorry and say something nice to him?'

said Esmeralda. 'I couldn't!' said Hortense, shocked. 'What would Miss Pincher say?' 'You'd feel so much better inside though,' said Esmeralda. 'Why don't you give it a try?' 'All right, I will,' said Hortense firmly.

At break time Hortense and Esmeralda went to find Henry Blob who was standing on his own in the playground.

'What do you want, skinny legs?' he said. Hortense was about to get angry and call him 'Fatty', but instead she decided to follow Esmeralda's advice.

'I just wanted to say I'm sorry Henry. I don't really think you're fat. I think you are big and strong and I was just saying it to please Miss Pincher so I could be top of the class.'

Henry was so shocked that he almost dropped the bun he was eating. 'That's all right, Hortense,' he eventually managed to gasp. 'I'm sorry I called you skinny legs. I was just cross. Do you want some of my bun?'

'Oh thank you Henry,' said Hortense without thinking. 'I love cherry buns. '

But Miss Scream had overheard the children talking. 'What, more sharing and children saying thank you and sorry! This is terrible. All of you off to the headmistress' office immediately.

'You too, girl,' she said, pointing to Esmeralda, who she realised was the culprit behind all this niceness. The three children hung their heads as Madam Groan, the headmistress, gave them a good telling off.

'Hortense and Henry. I am surprised at you. We have never had any trouble from you before. It must be Esmeralda's influence on you. You are both dismissed but I want a hundred lines from both of you by morning – 'I must not share and I must never say I am sorry.'

Now off you go both of you.'

And with a sympathetic look at Esmeralda the pair disappeared back to class where they were having a special session on the best places and times to pinch someone and make them cry.

Madam Groan looked severely at Esmeralda, 'As for you madam, I'm very disappointed with you. I only

accepted you here as a favour to your aunts but I can see that you are not going to fit in here. You obviously have a naturally good streak in your personality which will be very difficult to *eradicate**.

I can see that you will be a damaging influence on the other pupils here, if I allow you to remain. … Why Henry Blob has always been a selfish bully and Hortense a whining sneak, but after a morning in your company, they are both sharing and saying they are sorry. You are just too dangerous to have around any longer.

As a result, I have decided to expel you for the good of the school.

I will write to your aunts and explain why I am letting you go.'

And with that Esmeralda was given a letter to take back to Aunt Agatha and Aunt Hepzibah and shown off the premises.

Esmeralda couldn't believe it. She was so happy, she

skipped all the way home. She tried to look sorry as her aunts read the letter from Madam Groan explaining why they couldn't have her any longer at Witchthorn Academy.

'What are we going to do with you Esmeralda?' sighed Aunt Hepzibah. 'You really do need to go to school you know.' 'Well,'suggested Esmeralda, looking innocent. 'Perhaps I could go to the village school? It is so close by and I promise I will try and be a bit naughty and cause trouble in class if I can.'

Reluctantly her aunts agreed, although they doubted that Esmeralda would be able to keep her word. They sighed for they knew, however hard she tried, she couldn't help being good.

Chapter Four

Esmeralda and the
Readies Go Fundraising

Although she was a witch, Esmeralda was also a very keen Readie. But one day when she arrived at the village hall she found Chief Ladybird looking very sad.

'I'm afraid I've got some bad news for you girls,' said Chief Ladybird. 'Our funds are so low that we may have to close.'

The Readies *looked aghast**. Close down? Could it be possible?

'Isn't there anything we can do?' asked Esmeralda.

'I don't think so. We have lost our grant and we need to raise £400 by the end of the month to pay the council for the rent of the hall,' said Chief Ladybird, glumly.

'Couldn't we try and raise the money?' suggested Clare. 'We could do sponsored walks or jobs for people.'

Chief Ladybird started to look more cheerful. 'That's a

wonderful idea. It would be such a shame if we had to close.'

The girls all got into their groups to discuss what they would do. 'We could weed people's gardens,' suggested Angela. 'And we could wash cars,' said Clare.

'We could bake cakes and sell them,' said Esmeralda. She was very proud of the fairy cakes she had learnt to make at the Readies.

One of the girls from the Cricket pack lived on a farm. She decided to charge for rides on her pony. The Dragonfly pack decided to do a sponsored swim in the local pool.

When Esmeralda got home she told her aunts excitedly about their plans.

'I don't know why you want to go to all that trouble,' said Aunt Hepzibah. 'I could easily put a curse on the Council and then they would soon change their minds.'

'Oh don't do that, 'wailed

Esmeralda. She knew her aunt was trying to be helpful, but she didn't want her causing trouble. She thought all the fundraising plans sounded rather fun.

The next day Esmeralda got up early to make some fairy cakes. Her aunts were really a nuisance. They kept dropping into the kitchen and dipping their fingers into the mixture just to check that the taste was all right. Poor Esmeralda got quite ratty as she was worried that there wouldn't be enough left for the cakes.

Then to make matters worse she found that Aunt Hepzibah had used all the glace cherries and given them to her pet alligator Sam, for his elevenses.

'Oh no,' cried Esmeralda, who was getting very stressed. 'What am I going to do now?'

Neville, the magpie, saved the day however, by tracking down some wild strawberries from the wood, which looked even prettier and tasted even nicer.

Esmeralda felt very proud as she looked at the huge tray of delicious looking cakes. She just had to keep them out of Sam's way.

That afternoon she took the cakes to the stall that the Readies had set up in the village square.

The stall looked wonderful – full of all kinds of home made treats. Above it was a huge banner which said 'SUPPORT YOUR LOCAL READIES'.

Clare had brought with her a big red bucket full of water, a few bottles of washing up liquid and some old cloths.

She had made a sign which said, 'CAR WASH – ONLY £5'.

At first no one seemed interested. Then Mr Jones the butcher walked by.

'Will you girls clean my car. It's very dirty and a lot of work so I will give you £10?'

'Oh yes,' said Clare delightedly. Angela and Esmeralda went with her to inspect the car, which was parked behind his shop.

'You can use my hose-pipe,' said Mr Jones. 'It might be a good idea to go home and put some waterproofs on or you are going to get very wet.'

Esmeralda rushed home. She met Aunt Hepzibah in the hall and told her about the task. Poor Aunt Hepzibah was still feeling guilty about the cherries, so she decided she would help the girls. Imagine the girls' surprise when they got back to Mr Jones' yard to find his car all *gleaming* and shining.

Mr Jones came out very surprised. 'My goodness girls, I wouldn't have believed it. Have you finished already? How did you manage it?' And he gave them the promised £10.

Clare and Angela looked very puzzled but Esmeralda suspected what had happened. Aunt Hepzibah must had done a spell. She didn't know if she was pleased or disappointed.

The truth was Esmeralda had been rather looking forward to cleaning the car and using the hosepipe. It was much more fun feeling you'd really earned the money than just getting something for doing nothing.

'Well it looks like we won't be needing the hose or our waterproofs after all' said Clare disappointedly.

Fortunately at that moment, Brian from the garage passed by. 'You Readies look ready for action. How about coming to my garage and cleaning and polishing a few of my cars?'

The girls readily agreed. But this really was hard work. Even Neville the magpie and Sam the alligator came to help. By the time they had washed and polished two vans and five cars, Esmeralda was rather wishing she could remember some magic to help get the work done. But she was too tired to remember any spells at all.

Brian was so pleased with all their hard work that he gave them £50 and bought them all an ice cream each. 'I'm whacked,' said Clare as she licked her strawberry cone. 'Me too,' said Esmeralda.

'But it's a nice sort of tired isn't it?' she said, as she looked at all the gleaming cars in Brian's garage.

That evening all the Readies met at the Readie hut to find out how much money they had raised. Each pack brought what they had earned and put it in the big central pot.

The Bumble Bee pack, which Esmeralda and Angela and Clare belonged to had earned £127.50 through their cake stall and car washing. The Cricket pack's pony rides and cream teas at the farm had earned £87. The Dragon Fly's sponsored swim had earned £140 and the Beetle pack's weeding group £35.

'This means we are just £10.50 short of our target,' said Chief Ladybird delightedly.

At that moment there was a cough from the back. Everyone turned round. It was Aunt Hepzibah.

'Oh no,' thought Esmeralda, 'what is she up to now?'

But she needn't have worried. Aunt Hepzibah didn't usually approve of good deeds but she did want to help Esmeralda. 'Perhaps , you could sell this' she said.

Esmeralda couldn't believe it. It was the locket that Great, Great, Great, Great Uncle Horace had brought back from his gap year with pirates on the Spanish Main 300 years ago.'

Everyone clapped and applauded and Esmeralda felt very proud. Aunt Hepzibah tried hard not to look pleased, because that really wouldn't do for a scary witch. So she quickly turned herself into a bat and flew off.

The locket was indeed very valuable and once Mr Howard from the antique shop had examined it and sent it to London, enough money was raised not only to pay for the next quarter's rent, but for the whole year.

'Your Aunt Hepzibah tries hard to be horrid,' said Angela as they walked home, 'but I think you are a good influence on her. She's starting to be really nice. Just like you Esmeralda.'

Chapter Five

Esmeralda Tidies Up

Esmeralda was feeding Sidney the spider in the kitchen with his favourite dead bluebottle snack, when Aunt Agatha came in. She was very angry.

'I have just been in your bedroom, Esmeralda,' she said, 'and it's a disgrace!' Esmeralda looked at her feet.

'How many times have I told you, to keep things untidy! But Oh No! You have to tidy everything away and fold up all your clothes and put all your spell books back on the shelves! It is all very well to dust and clean up all those cobwebs. But have you thought about all the hard work that Sidney and his friends do, spinning those cobwebs, and then with the flick of the duster you undo it?'

Esmeralda sighed. She was used to being told off about the state of her bedroom. But she couldn't help it. She liked to see things nice and tidy. It made her feel calm and it was so much easier to find things, when everything had their proper place.

'Come upstairs' said Aunt Agatha, 'I am fed up with having to untidy your room. It's about time you learnt to do it yourself. You are a big girl now. Go and untidy all the tidiness you have created. I will come and inspect it when you have finished. And as a punishment instead of using your spell book to make it untidy, you are going to have to do it all yourself.' 'And take down that dreadful poster,' she added. 'In my day we had scary posters of vampires and werewolves, not men in brown dresses.'

Esmeralda hated being in trouble with her aunts and wanted to be obedient, but she couldn't help it. She liked being tidy.

'Take Sidney with you,' continued her aunt. 'I want nice strong cobwebs in all the corners and over the windows and plenty of dirt in the corners so the cockroaches have somewhere to live.'

Sidney needed no second command and quickly scuttled across the floor and hopped into the safety of Esmeralda's pocket and the pair of them climbed up the stairs to Esmeralda's bedroom.

She had to admit it was very tidy, with everything neatly tidied away.

'I am so sorry for getting you into trouble, Sidney,' said Esmeralda, giving him the last of the bluebottles. 'We will play later.'

The pair of them worked really hard for the next couple of hours. Sidney spun six strong cobwebs with the help of his friend Alfred, who lived in the attic, and Esmeralda went back and forth into the garden, getting her shoes really dirty and then *grinding** the mud into the carpet.

She had stacked away all the back issues of 'Spells magazine', which Aunt Hepzibar loved, in date order in a nice pile. Now she had to find random places for them all. She bent down and pushed some under the bed and a few behind the radiator and scattered the rest on the floor round the room. She then went downstairs to find some dirty cups to bring upstairs and create nice circular stains on the chest of drawers. Then she knocked one full cup of bat's blood cordial on the carpet, which left a nice big mark.

Finally everything was suitably untidy, and Aunt Agatha came and gave it her approval. 'That's much better, Esmeralda,' she said. 'Just keep it like this.'

It was always such a battle, thought Esmeralda. She couldn't wait for the time when she would be old enough to have her own house, which she could keep as neat and tidy as she wanted.

At that moment, the door bell rang. It was Angela and Clare who had come to see if Esmeralda could come out and play.

'Well,' said Aunt Agatha grumpily, 'Esmeralda has untidied her room now, so I suppose she can go out. But be sure to misbehave Esmeralda! I don't want to hear from people that you have been kind and helpful when you are out.'

'I'll do my best,' said Esmeralda, but she knew she couldn't help being kind and helpful which was why she was always getting into trouble.

Angela was upset. 'I'm fed up of living at home. My mum is always shouting at me and my sister. She used to be nice and calm but now she seems to be angry all the time.'

'Maybe she is just tired,' said Esmeralda, as she knew that Angela's father was in hospital and Angela's mother was looking after Angela and her sister Dawn, all on her own.'

'Let's go and cheer your mother up,' said Esmeralda. 'How?' said Angela.

'I don't know,' replied Esmeralda. 'Let's go and see what we can do to help. We are Readies after all. And Readies always do good deeds.'

So the three little girls set off for Angela's house. When they arrived there was a note on the table for Angela from her mother saying that she taken Angela's sister and they gone to visit her father in the local hospital.

Esmeralda noticed that the house was very untidy. There were lots of dirty dishes in the sink, and the kitchen floor was very muddy. Her aunts would have loved it like that, but Esmeralda knew that most mothers liked things tidy, like she did.

'Why don't we tidy up the kitchen,' she said. 'So when your mother comes back everything is nice and tidy?'

'She would be pleased' said Angela. Angela had thought about doing something before but it seemed such a big task and it was such a sunny day that she had decided it would be nicer to go out and play with Clare and Esmeralda.

But what fun they had washing the dishes together. Esmeralda stood on a box and filled the sink with hot soapy water, while Clare dried the plates and Angela put them away as she knew where all the crockery went.

When this was all done Clare found the big brush under the stairs, and they swept the floor. 'We could wash it too,' said Esmeralda and between them they found a bucket and mop.

'What about the sitting room?' said Esmeralda.

It was so much more fun doing things together, thought Angela. She remembered all the times she had left her mother to do everything herself, not even taking her plate into the kitchen and instead, going out to play. No wonder her mother used to get upset at times.

Soon the sitting room was also lovely and tidy too. Sidney had a word with the resident house spider, Alfonse, who was a cousin of Alfred the spider in their attic. He suggested that Alfonse come and live at Esmeralda's house where there was plenty of work for him to do, and where he would be much more welcome than at Angela's house. Alfonse agreed.

'We could make a cake too', said Angela. 'Mum loves cake.' 'Me too,' said Clare, who loved sweet things.

'I have never made a cake before,' said Esmeralda.

'Me neither,' said Angela. 'But I have seen my mother

make one. She uses one of Jammy Johnson's recipe books on the shelf there.

Between them the girls got down the recipe book and flicked through the pages. There were so many to choose from: Chocolate, Strawberry and Fresh Cream, Ginger and Lemon. They decided that the Strawberry Gateaux looked the nicest.

'So what do we need to make it?' said Esmeralda, taking the lead.

'Flour, sugar,' recited Clare going down the list. 'Yes, We have those in the cupboard,' said Angela.

'Eggs?' 'No.' said Angela, disappointed. 'There don't seem to be any left.'

'I know where there are some,' said Clare. 'The hens from Wiley's farm are always wandering into our garden and they sometimes lay eggs there. I will dash home and I will also ask my grandfather for some strawberries from his allotment,' and with that she disappeared out of the house.

'I know where we can get some cream,' said Esmeralda, remembering that Aunt Hepzibah had been practising *curdling** that morning and had left some cream in the pail in the shed.

By the time Clare and Esmeralda had got back, Angela was busy creaming the butter and sugar together till it was white and soft almost like cream. The difficult part was cracking the eggs.

'I have never done it before,' said Angela, 'my mum doesn't normally let me in case I get shell in the cake mixture. But I've seen her do it lots of times, so I am sure I can do it.' She hit the egg on the side of the bowl. But, Oh dear, it was harder than it looked! And the broken egg slipped to the floor. 'Oh no!' said Angela.

'Don't worry,' said Clare, 'I have brought plenty of eggs with me. My grandfather gave me a whole box and we only need three.' 'Yes,' said Esmeralda encouragingly, 'Just try again'.

Angela's second attempt also went *awry**, much to her dog, Angus', delight, who soon hoovered both eggs up. But the third time she tried, she did a perfect break and got the egg into the bowl, and then after that it was easy.

'I know how to break eggs. I know how to break eggs', said Angela triumphantly.

Clare then sieved in the flour and carefully blended it in, as she had seen Jammy Johnson do on the television.

While the cake was cooking in the oven the three girls washed and *hulled the strawberries** and whipped the cream.

'This is such fun,' said Clare as they put a tablecloth on

the table, and some fresh flowers in a vase. 'Your mother is going to be so happy,' said Esmeralda.

And so she was. When Angela's mother came she couldn't believe what she saw. She left the house in such a mess and was *bracing herself** to come back and tidy things up, but instead everything was spotless and the most delicious strawberry cake was there on the table.

'What has happened?' she said, 'Is this magic?'

'No.' said Angela, pleased. 'We did it. And I know how to break eggs now!' She decided it would probably be better not to mention about the eggs that were now in Angus' tummy.

'My darling girl', said Angela's mother, hugging her. 'What wonderful girls you Readies are!' The girls *beamed**. When Esmeralda arrived home, she was still smiling.

'Why are you smiling in that *smug** way, Esmeralda? Have you been good again?' 'Not too good,' said Esmeralda as she sat down to supper.

She did try to be bad, but it was just so difficult and so much more fun being good!

Wonder Words

Granny Maud, to whom this book is dedicated, is Swedish. She always loved expanding her vocabulary of English words and would often ask the family what they meant exactly. Sometimes we didn't know and we would then have to look them up in the dictionary or thesaurus.

The English language has some great words, which we don't use enough! It is just as easy to learn interesting words as boring words.

Here are some alternatives to the words I have used in these stories which you might like to try out instead. They mean almost the same but not quite! Which do you think feels best and would you rather use?

Chapter One
Esmeralda Wants To Be A Readie

page 2: **in unison** = together, in chorus, in synchronization, simultaneously.

page 4: **thoroughly** unpleasant = extremely, exceedingly, singularly, uncommonly, abominably.

page 8: **sneaked** into the house = crept, tiptoed, furtively entered, slinked, clandestinely entered.

page 10: **thirst quenching** = thirst slaking, thirst assuaging.

page 10: **plumping** their pillows = puffing up.

Chapter Two
Esmeralda and the Beauty Spells

page 13: **made a grimace** - scowled, gave a peevish look, frowned, looked askance.

page 13: **scampering** - running about, scurrying around,

page 14: **intrigued** - curious, fascinated, captivated, tantalised.

page 16: **interjected** - added, butted in, interposed.

page 16: **enticed** - coaxed, tempted, inveigled.

page 16: **different hues** - different shades or colours.

page 22: **quizzically** - enquiringly, interrogatively, probingly, searchingly.

Chapter Three
Esmeralda is Expelled

page 27: **mused** - pondered, reflected, thought about, mulled over.

page 30: **incorrigibly** good - resolutely, tenaciously, uncompromisingly.

page 32: **the audacity** - boldness, nerve, fearlessness, daring.

page 37: **eradicate** - blot out, suppress, root out, erase, get rid of.

Chapter Four
Esmeralda Goes Fundraising

page 41: **looked aghast** - horrified, disconcerted, disturbed.

page 45: **gleaming** - shining, sparkling, shimmering.

Chapter Five
Esmeralda Tidies Up

page 53: **grinding** - rubbing in, crushing, pressing, mashing.

page 60: **curdling** - turning milk or cream sour and thick.

page 61: **hulled the strawberries** - removed the green top of strawberry.

page 62: **bracing herself** - preparing herself, gearing herself up, getting herself ready.

page 62: **beamed** - smiled, gave a big smile, grinned.

page 62: **smug** - demure, pleased with herself, innocent.

page 61: **awry -** askew, amiss.

The Little Witch Who Wanted To Be Good

Children's Recommendations

I really enjoyed writing *The Little Witch Who Wanted to be Good* but I wasn't sure if it would appeal to children, so I sent the first three Esmeralda stories I wrote to a local school, Eaton House, The Manor Girls' School in Clapham.

Miss Kirsten's class F3 very kindly gave me their feedback. This was extremely positive and I realised that the children got my humour and the message, which was very encouraging.

This kept me going over the following years as I tried to find the right illustrator and to get the book published.

Here below are some of the children's comments, which I thought you might enjoy:

'I enjoyed the story and I really want to hear it again.' Lottie (8)

'I thought it made me feel as if I was really seeing it happen. I loved it.' Minxie (8)

'I think it was the best story I ever heard! I absolutely loved it!' Laura (8)

'It was really good. I loved it. I disliked nothing, nothing 1,000,000/1,000,000.' Eleanor (8)

'I would like to hear it again. I really liked this book. It makes me want to do good deeds.' Robyn (8)

'I loved it, I want one. One of the best books I have ever read.' Maddie (8)

'I loved the story about Esmeralda. I would like to read it ten times again. I loved the story about the fundraising. I would like to have it at home. My best part was when they were helping to clean cars, and sell things.' Anya (8)

'I like it. I would like to hear it again. I liked the bit when the aunt had to be more important than the other one.' Isobel (8)

'I liked it when Esmeralda helped her aunts when they were sick.'

'I think my favourite bit was when they cleaned the cars'.

Do You Want To Be A Readie
Like Esmeralda?

1. Read the Readie Promise every day:

I promise to always be ready
to be generous, kind, honest,
cheerful and courageous.
I promise to help others,
to love God and serve
my community.

2. Make a list of good deeds that you can do to help others and write them in an exercise book:

- make a cup of tea for someone
- help with the washing up
- draw a card for a sick person
- share your sweets/toys
- don't gossip or say nasty things about people
- say a prayer for someone who is ill
- give some of your pocket money to someone in need
- come up with your own good deed

3. Tick off the good deeds you do every day. When you have reached a 100 you are a proper Readie!

(If you would like ladybird stickers to help you keep a record of your good deeds get in touch with us at: LittleWitchWhoWantedToBeGood@gmail.com and we can send you 100 ladybird stickers for £2.50+85p p/p)

REMEMBER READIES ALWAYS HAVE FUN AND ARE ALWAYS READY TO HELP OTHERS!

For more books or information about Esmeralda and the Readies email Kristina Cooper at:
LittleWitchWhoWantedToBeGood@gmail.com

About The Authors

KRISTINA COOPER is a journalist who edited the Good News magazine for many years. She has been writing and telling stories since she was seven years old but this is her first children's book.

JESSICA COOPER, who is Kristina's niece, is a British fashion designer living and working in Sweden. She has always loved hearing the Little Witch stories and felt inspired to illustrate the book.

Further copies of this book can be obtained from
Goodnews Books, Upper Level, St John's Church,
296 Sundon Park Road, Luton, Beds LU3 3AL

www.goodnewsbooks.co.uk
orders@goodnewsbooks.co.uk
tel: 01582 571011

Correspondence with the author
should be directed to

LittleWitchWhoWantedToBeGood@gmail.com